By Bill Atkins

How Grandad Elf lost his pointy ears

Copyright © 2022 Bill Atkins

Published by North Pole Trading Post.
ISBM: 9798428578058
For more copies of this book please contact:
grandadelfnorthpole@gmail.com
Tel: (+4) 07876 574 313
Designed & set by Sammy C Brooks

Tagalong and Scruffy

Grandad Elf's Job List

1. look after Tagalong

2. make coin boxes

3. meet the children for me

Thanks
Father Christmas

Grandad Elf is Santa's best friend.
At 5 feet 3 inches, he's quite a tall old elf.

He lives at the North Pole with two dogs,
his old little dog named "Scruffy" and
Santa's dog, "Tagalong".
Tagalong's job is to guard the sleigh on
Christmas Eve, when Santa's delivering
the presents to all the children.

Grandad Elf now has three jobs up at the North Pole. His first job is to look after Tagalong; his second job is to make little boxes, all by hand, for Santa's special coin presents.

Grandad Elf's third job is a very important job: it's to stand in for Santa on certain occasions when Santa is otherwise busy.

Nikki &
Grandad Elf

Hugo

Grandad Elf loves his jobs and even performs some magic too, which he learnt from a very magical elf named Nikki. Now, Grandad Elf isn't the Head Elf, no, no, no! That's Hugo, but Grandad Elf is Santa's best friend.

One day, in February 1955, up at the North Pole, when Grandad Elf was out walking with Scruffy, Santa's dog Tagalong and two of his friends, Elfiedoodles – she's the elf who runs the Elf Academy – and Pom Pom the Elf,

Elfiedoodles & PomPom

as they were walking along some naughty older teenagers decided to throw lots of snowballs at them. But Grandad Elf was old, so he wasn't very quick to bend down and pick up the snow and throw snowballs back at them.

"Help!" he shouted, but no one heard.

Elfiedoodles and Pom Pom the Elf ran off to fetch help, but by this time there were around ten children all throwing more snowballs at Grandad Elf, many of the snowballs hitting his pointed ears and making them sore and very cold – so cold and sore they got damaged.

Frosty the elf

NORTH POLE

But as luck would have it, along came Buddy the Elf. He was very tall, even taller than Frosty the Elf.

Buddy was the best in the North Pole at making and throwing snowballs. He was so fast.

Buddy is always going to New York in America and throwing snowballs there in Central Park.

Elves Patch and Groober came to help too, and the naughty children finally ran away. But Grandad Elf's ears were hurting, and were very sore, so when Santa got to hear about it, he banned throwing snowballs at anybody's head. Forever.

"Don't wory, there will be NO MORE throwing snowballs at anybody's head!!"

Grandad Elf had to have an operation on his ears to remove the points, but luckily, they healed up nicely and that's how Grandad Elf lost his Pointy Ears.

Grandad Elf has a very good friend called Keith the Elf. He's very clever and made some nice things for Grandad Elf to cheer him up.

Grandad Elf was really pleased. Also, he was given a very special clock for long service from Santa.

Sometimes Grandad Elf gets permission to Help Father Christmas deliver the presents on Christmas Eve and Tagalong always goes along and guards the Sleigh.

Grandad Elf

February 1955

February 2022

So, now you know.
That's how Grandad Elf lost his pointed ears. And remember, never throw snowballs at someone's head, as it's very dangerous and you, too, could lose your pointy ears!

Dear Father Christmas

For Christmas this year I would really like for Christmas.

- ~~guitar~~
- guitar (electric or acoustic) I don't mind
- 21 inch TV   • money
- Copic Markers
- Lego
- A boyfriend
- A puppy

I think the last one is impossible but who knows maybe I will get a boyfriend this Christmas.

PS: Tell Grandad elf I would really like some money or a puppy for Christmas.

Sophie Lawton

Grandad Elf's
Photos

Grandad Elf meeting some of his friends

Add your photo with Grandad Elf

Merry Christmas